WELCOME TO
PASSPORT TO READING
A beginning reader's ticket to a brand-new world!

Every book in this program is designed to build read-along and read-alone skills, level by level, through engaging and enriching stories. As the reader turns each page, he or she will become more confident with new vocabulary, sight words, and comprehension.

These PASSPORT TO READING levels will help you choose the perfect book for every reader.

READING TOGETHER
Read short words in simple sentence structures together to begin a reader's journey.

READING OUT LOUD
Encourage developing readers to sound out words in more complex stories with simple vocabulary.

READING INDEPENDENTLY
Newly independent readers gain confidence reading more complex sentences with higher word counts.

READY TO READ MORE
Readers prepare for chapter books with fewer illustrations and longer paragraphs.

This book features sight words from the educator-supported Dolch Sight Words List. This encourages the reader to recognize commonly used vocabulary words, increasing reading speed and fluency.

For more information, please visit passporttoreadingbooks.com.

Enjoy the journey!

Little, Brown and Company

Hachette Book Group
1290 Avenue of the Americas, New York, NY 10104
Visit us at lb-kids.com

Little, Brown and Company is a division of Hachette Book Group, Inc.
The Little, Brown name and logo are trademarks of Hachette Book Group, Inc.

The publisher is not responsible for websites (or their content)
that are not owned by the publisher.

First Edition: May 2016

Library of Congress Control Number: 2015954821

ISBN 978-0-316-26723-6

10 9 8 7 6 5 4 3 2 1

CW

Printed in the United States of America

Passport to Reading titles are leveled by independent reviewers applying the
standards developed by Irene Fountas and Gay Su Pinnell in *Matching Books to
Readers: Using Leveled Books in Guided Reading*, Heinemann, 1999.

TEEN TITANS GO!™

PIZZA POWER

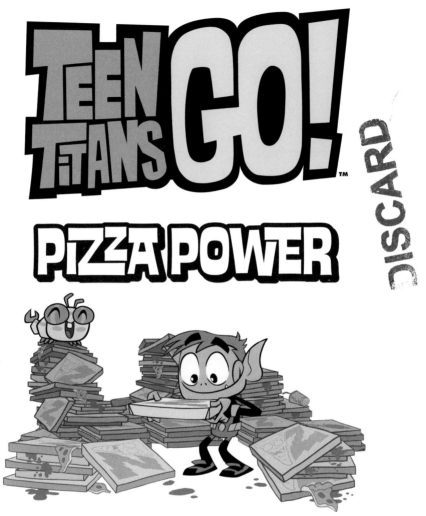

Adapted by Jennifer Fox

Based on the episode “Hey Pizza”

Written by Amy Wolfram

Based on the episode “Truth, Justice, and What?”

Written by Michael Jelenic and Aaron Horvath

LB

LITTLE, BROWN AND COMPANY

New York Boston

Attention, Teen Titans fans!
Look for these words when you read
this book. Can you spot them all?

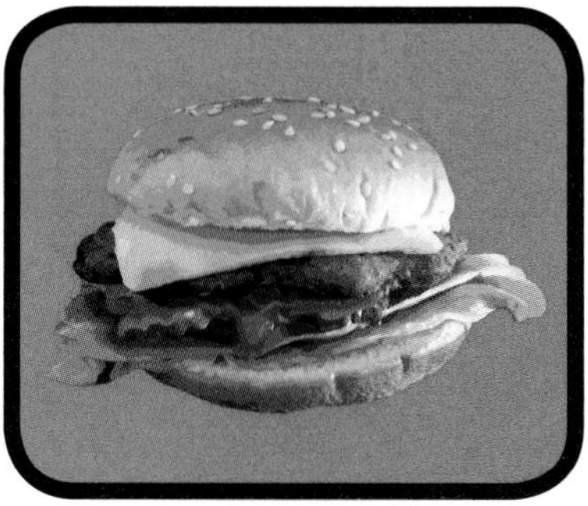

burger

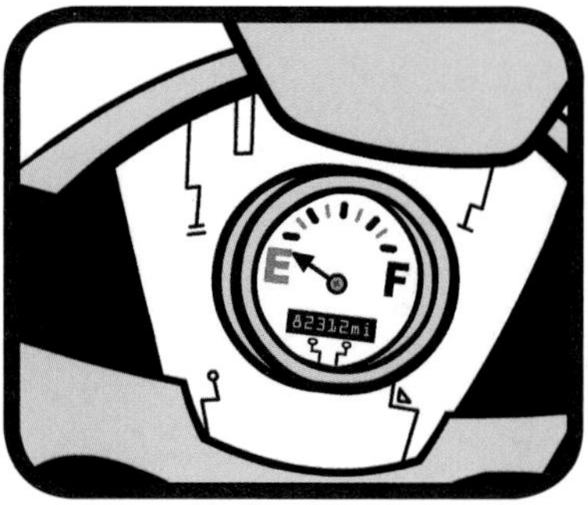
E
F

tank

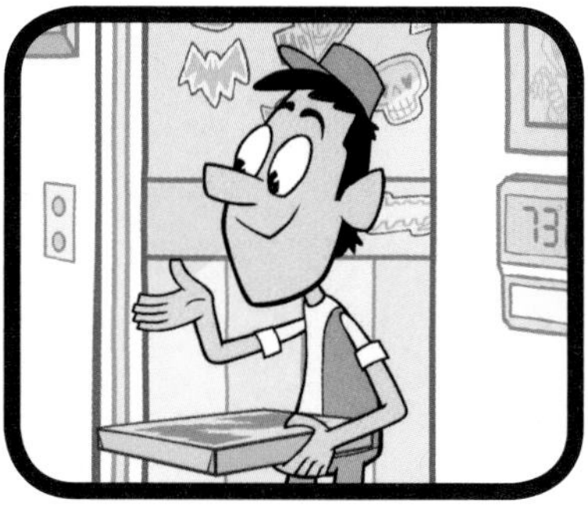

pizza guy

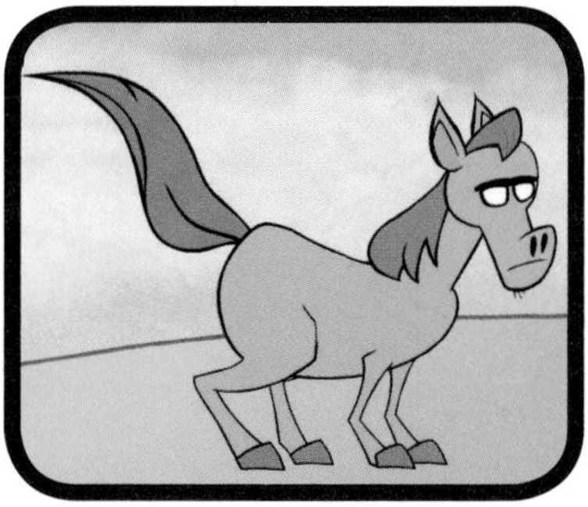

pony

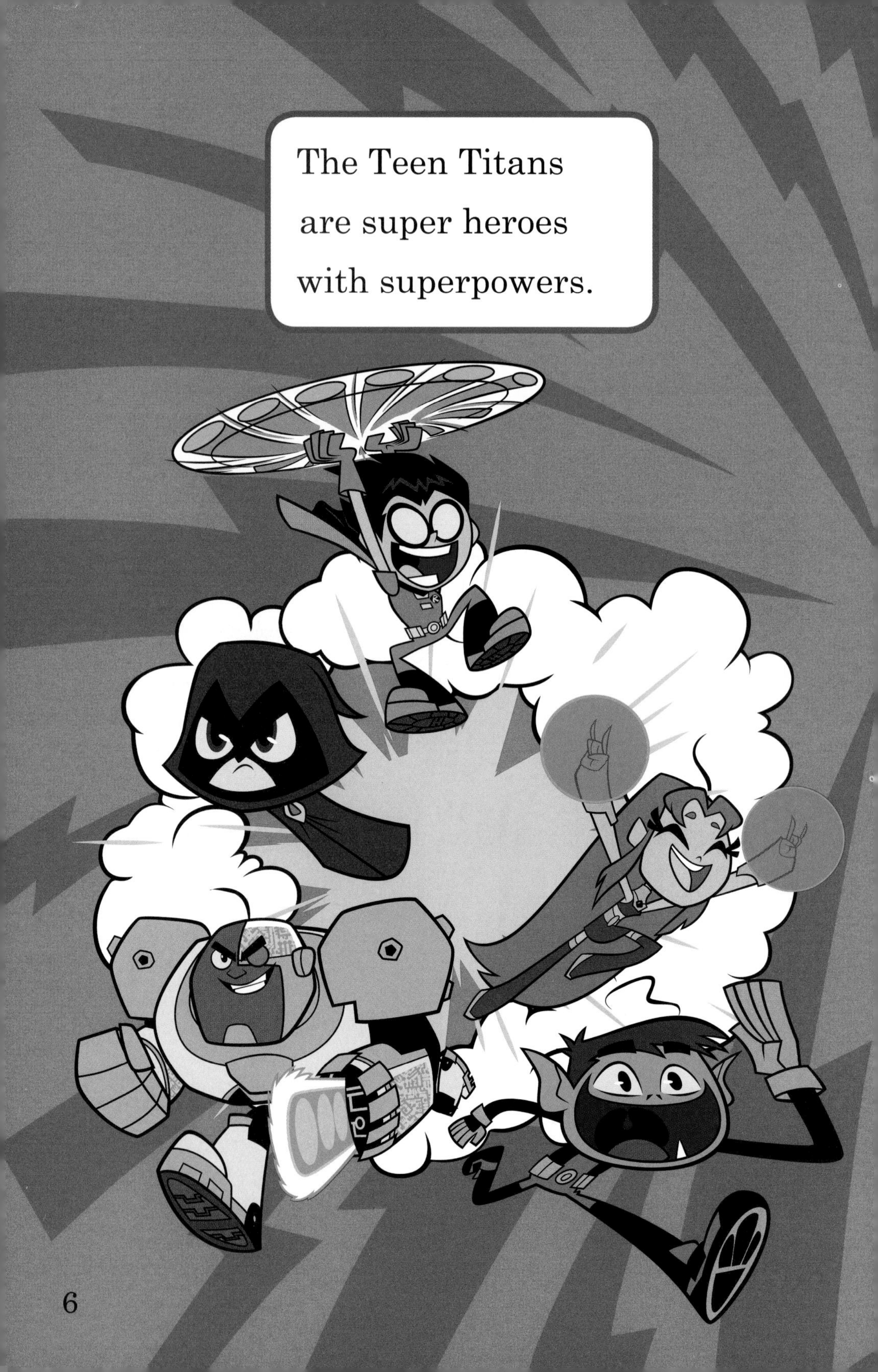

The Teen Titans
are super heroes
with superpowers.

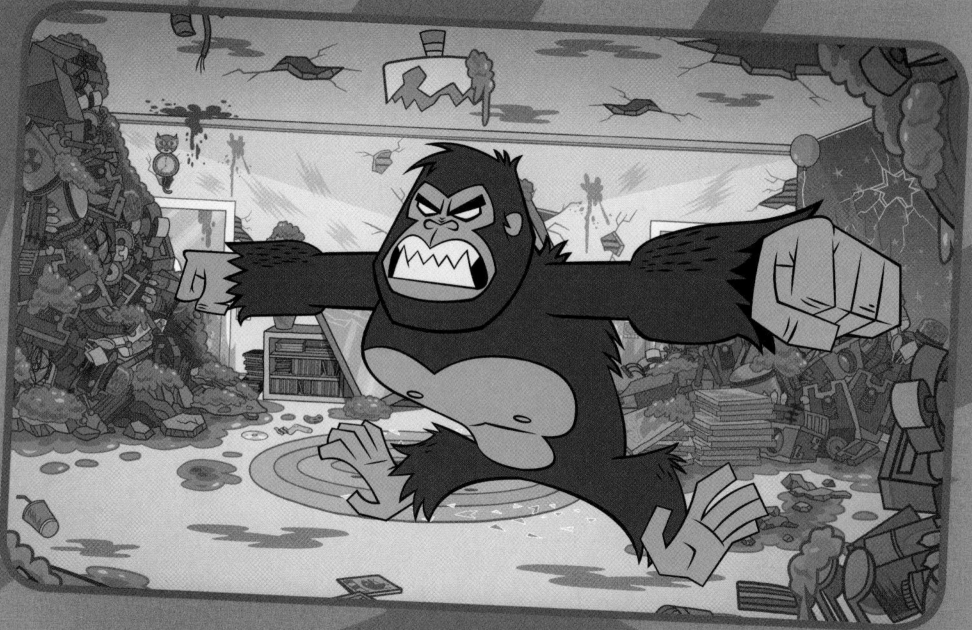

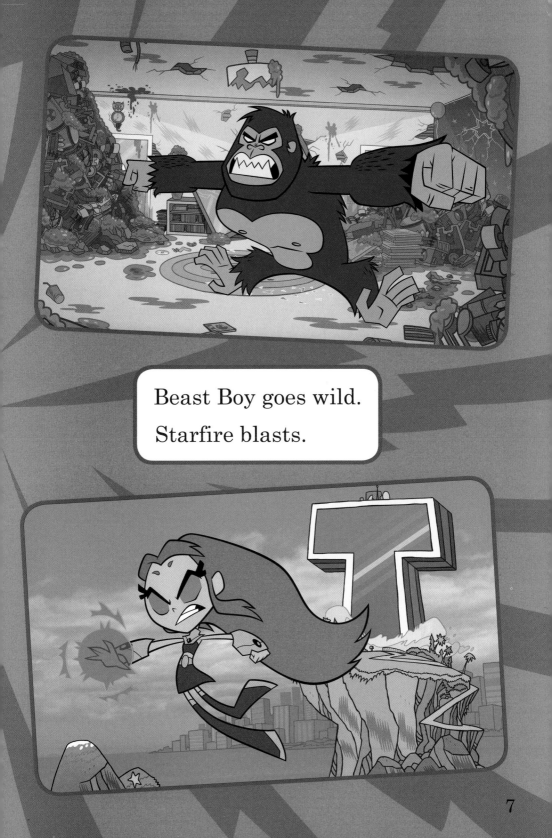

Beast Boy goes wild.
Starfire blasts.

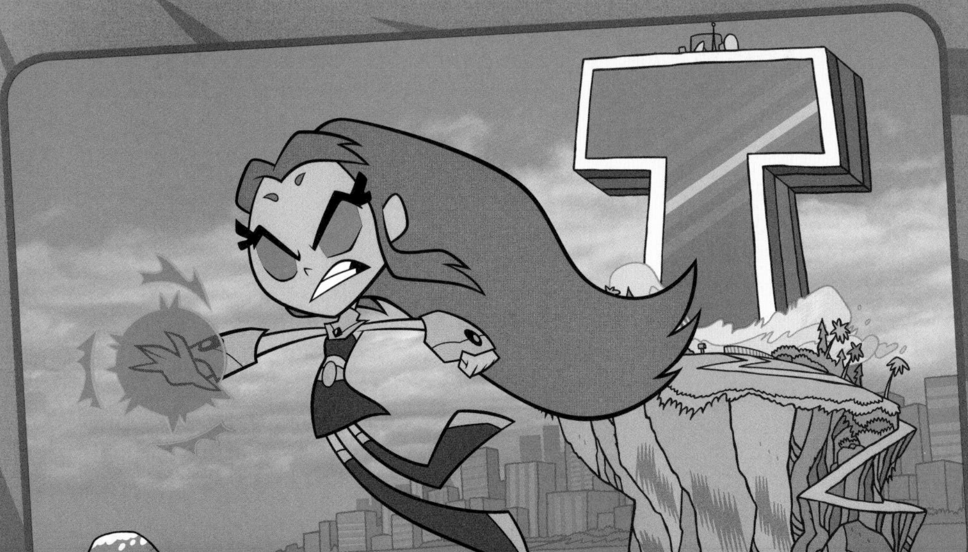

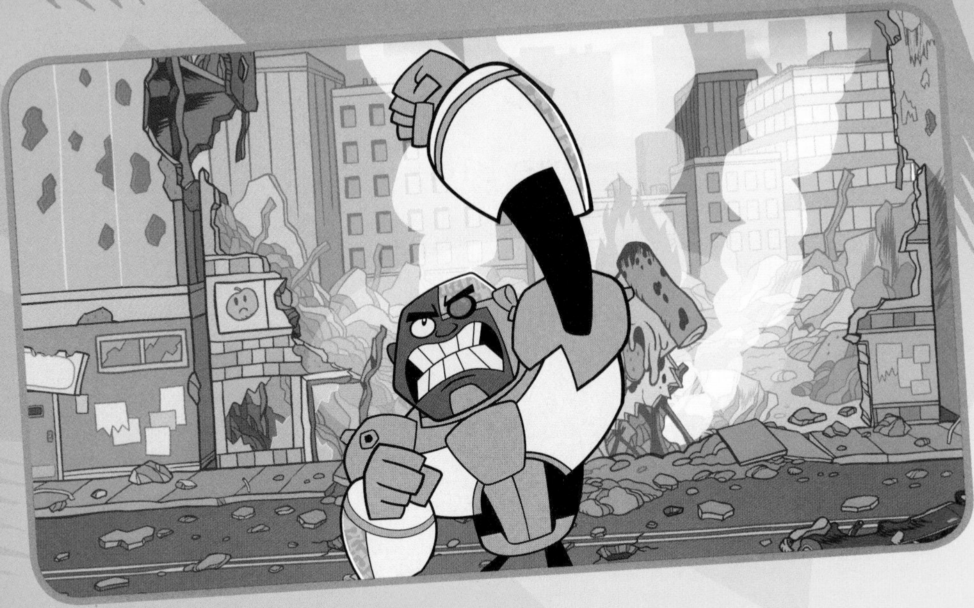

Cyborg smashes.
Raven casts spells.

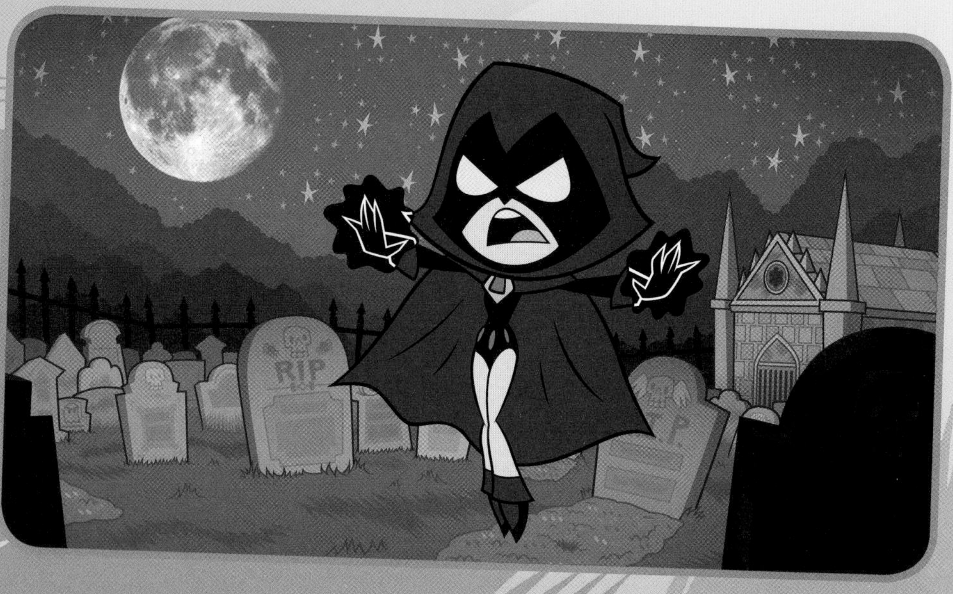
RIP

And Robin?
No one knows
what he does.

What gives the Teen Titans
their powers?
Is it magic?

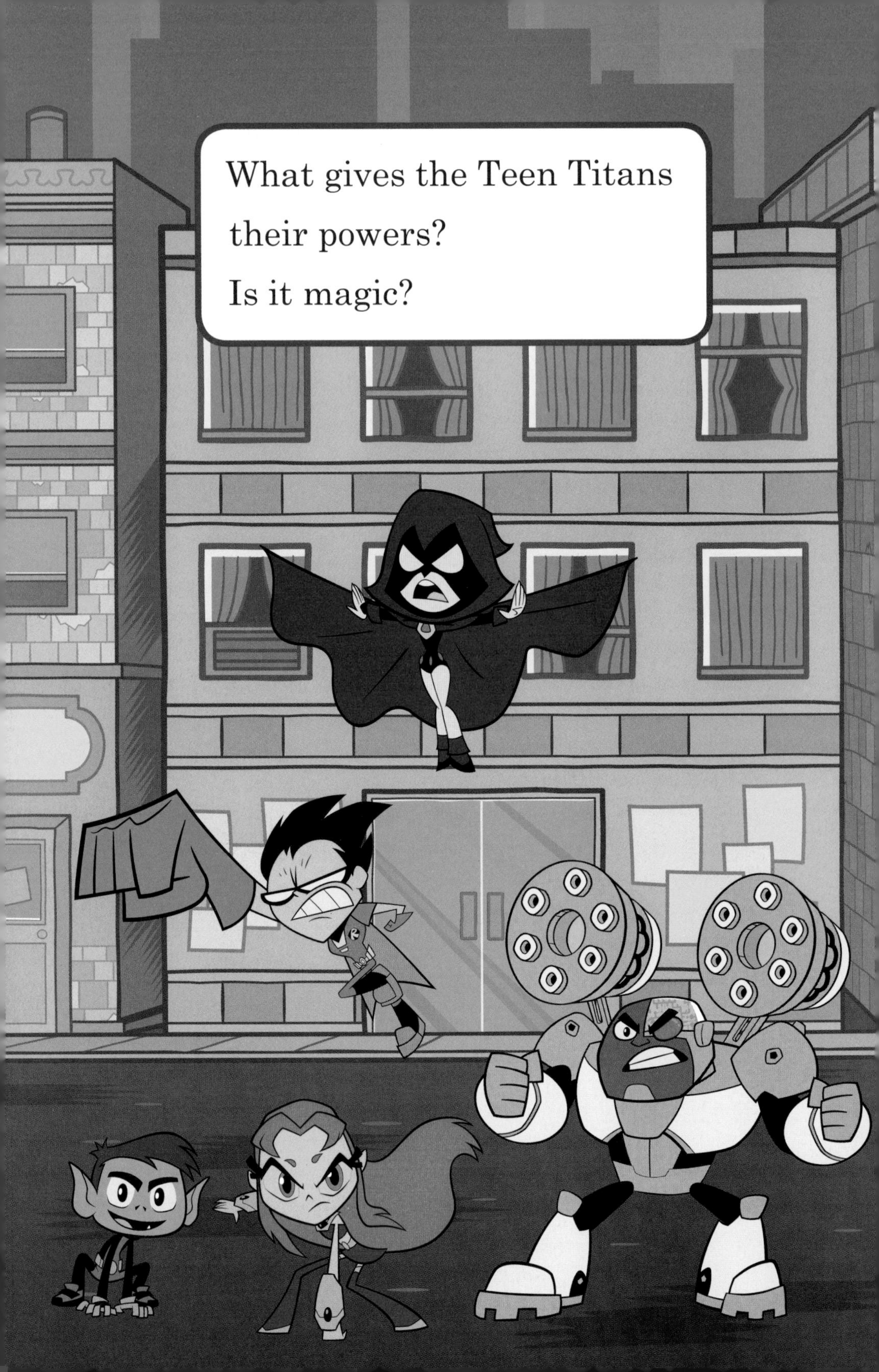

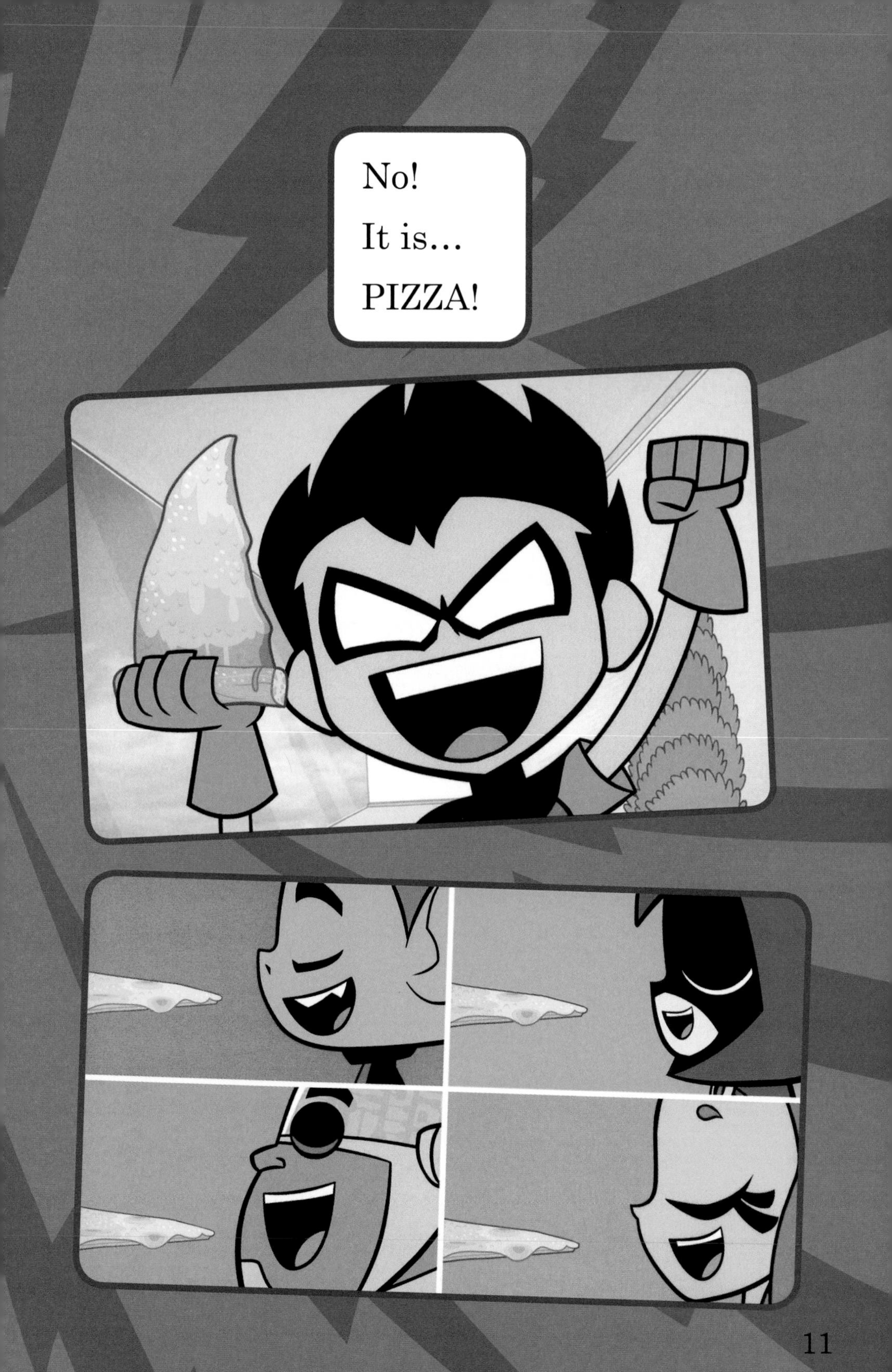
No!
It is...
PIZZA!

They eat it for breakfast, lunch, and dinner! They eat it all day, anytime!

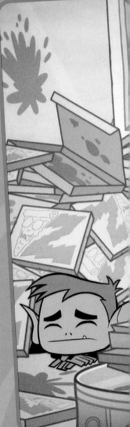

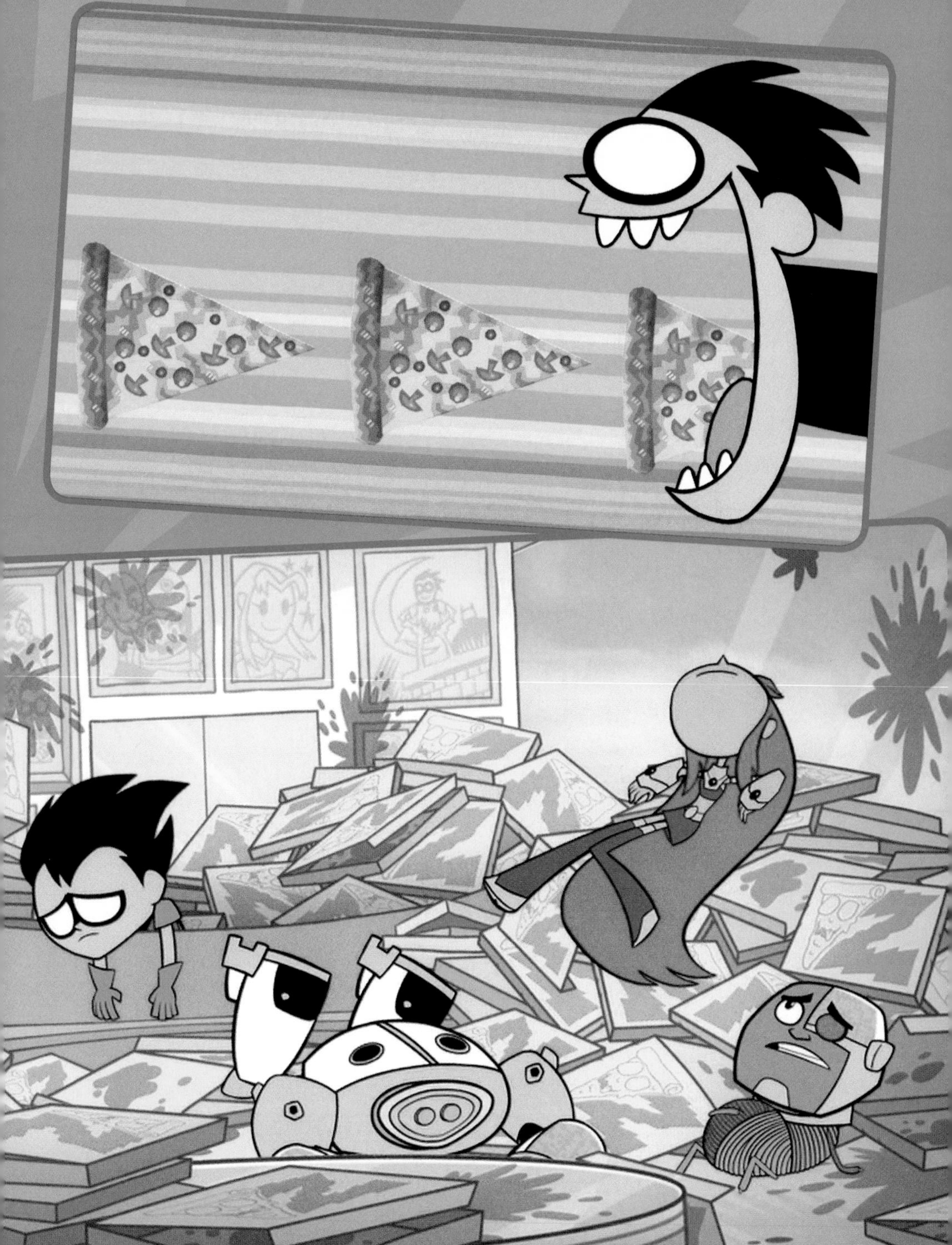

Burgers are beefy.

Burritos are zesty.

But hot, gooey pizza
is the best...

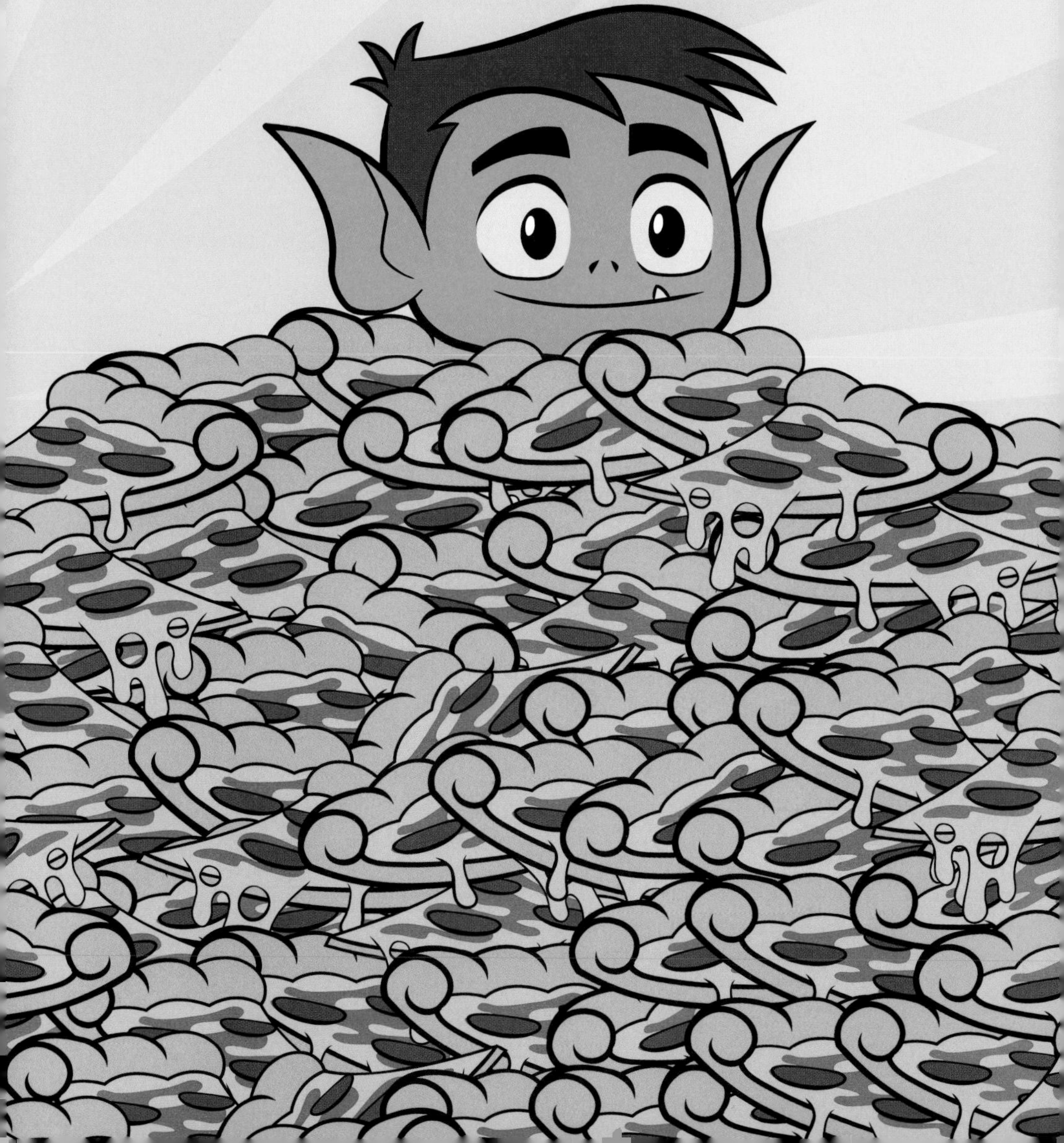

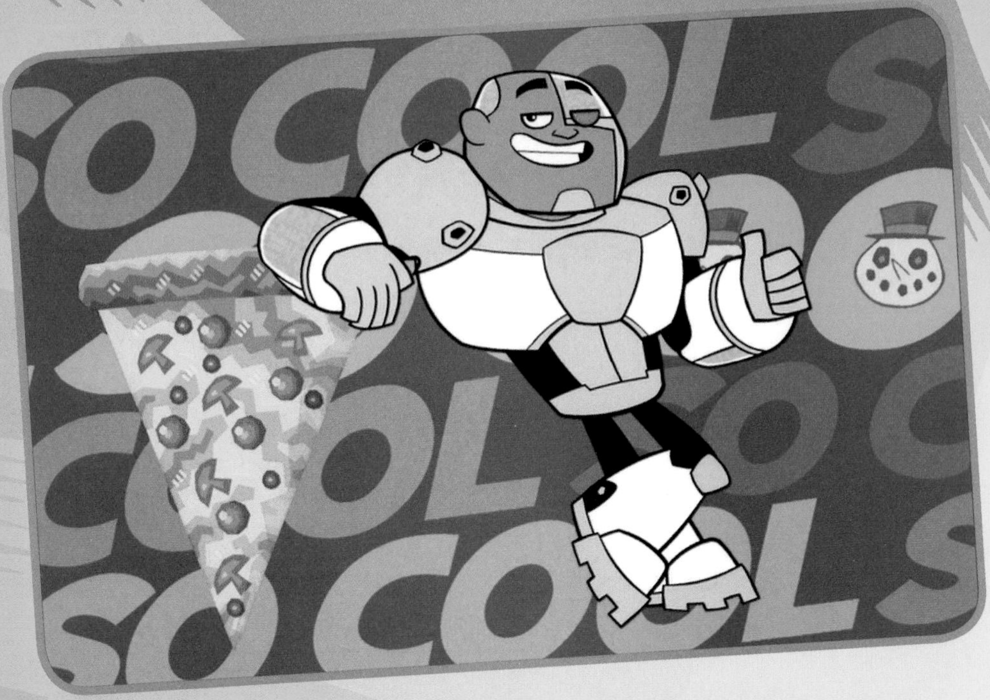
SO COOL

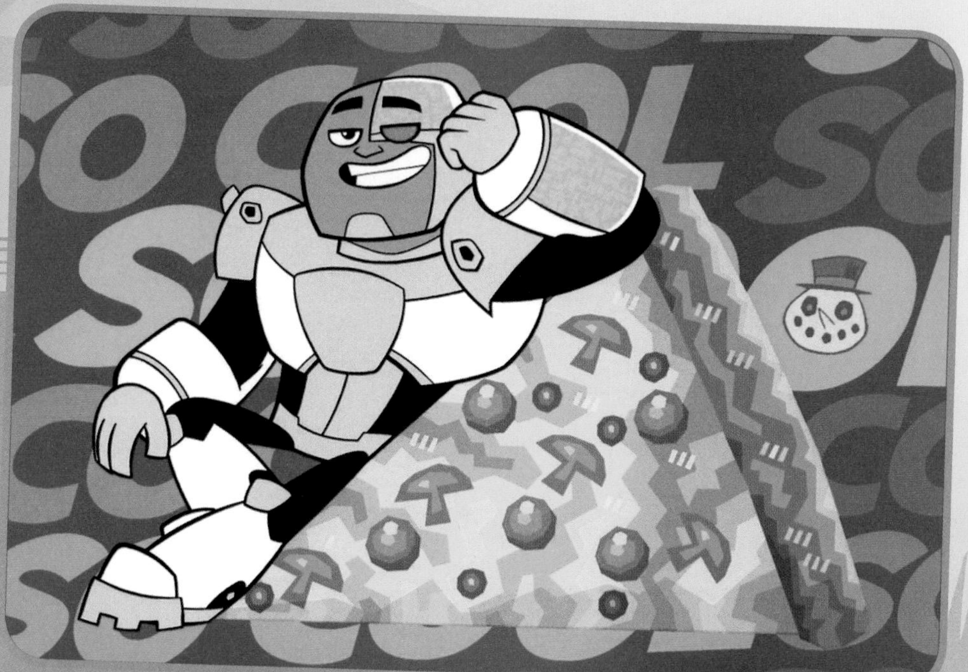
SO COOL

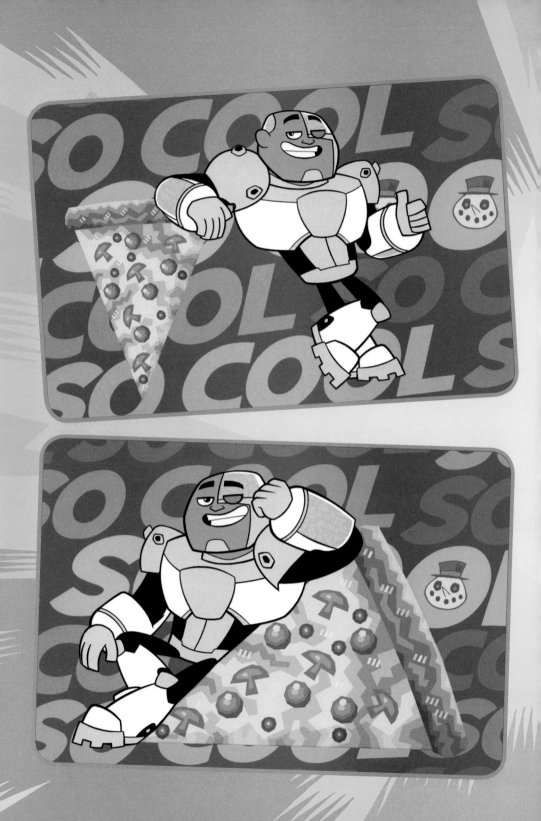

...any way
you slice it.

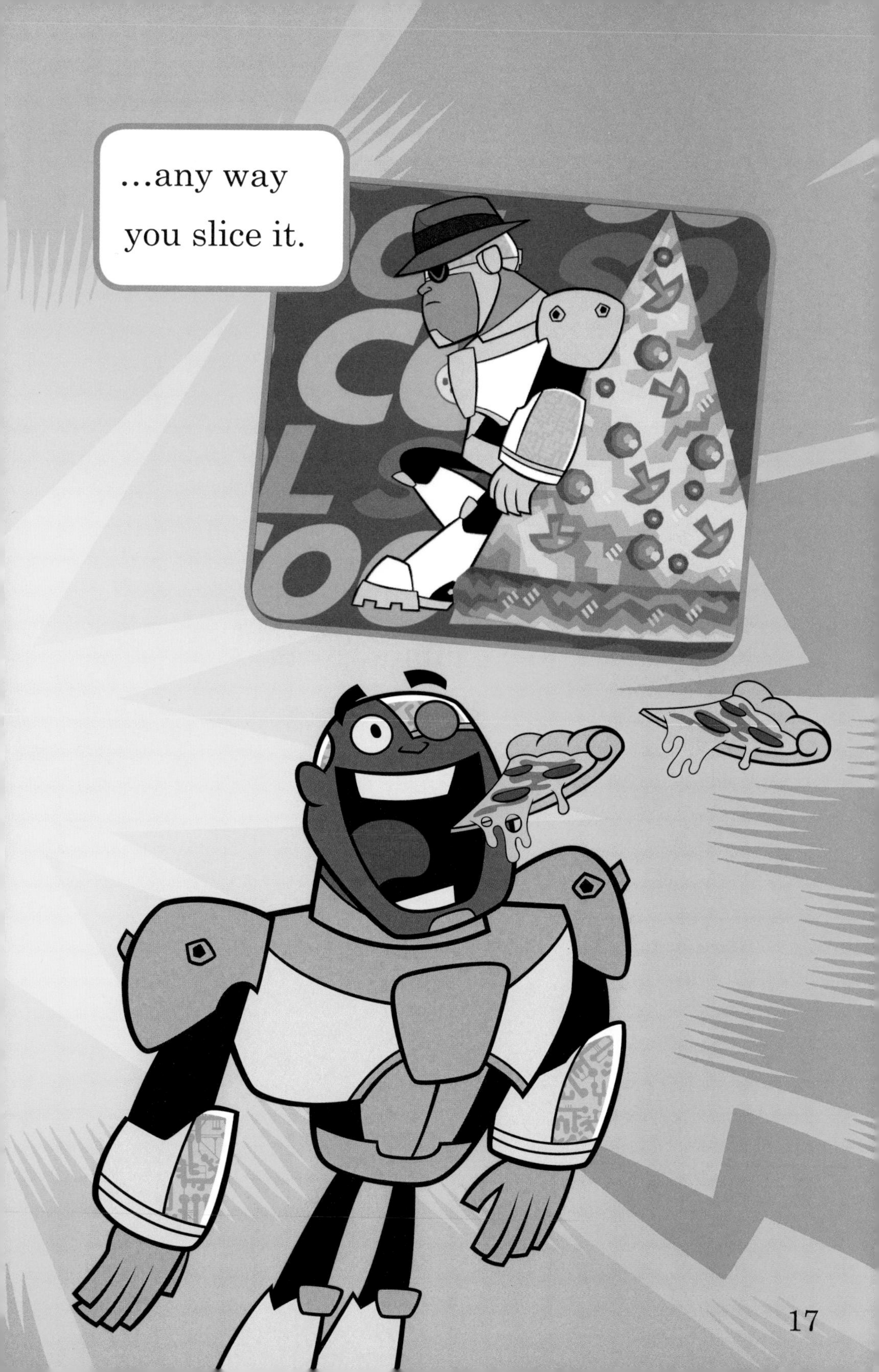

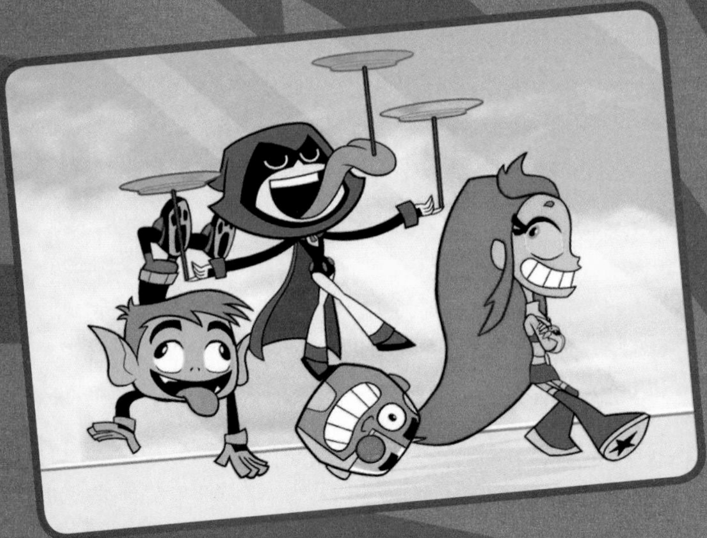

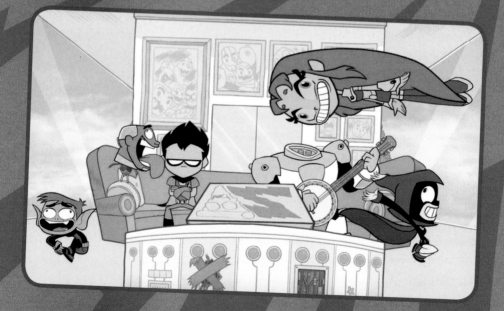

It makes you
dance, jump,
burp, and go crazy!

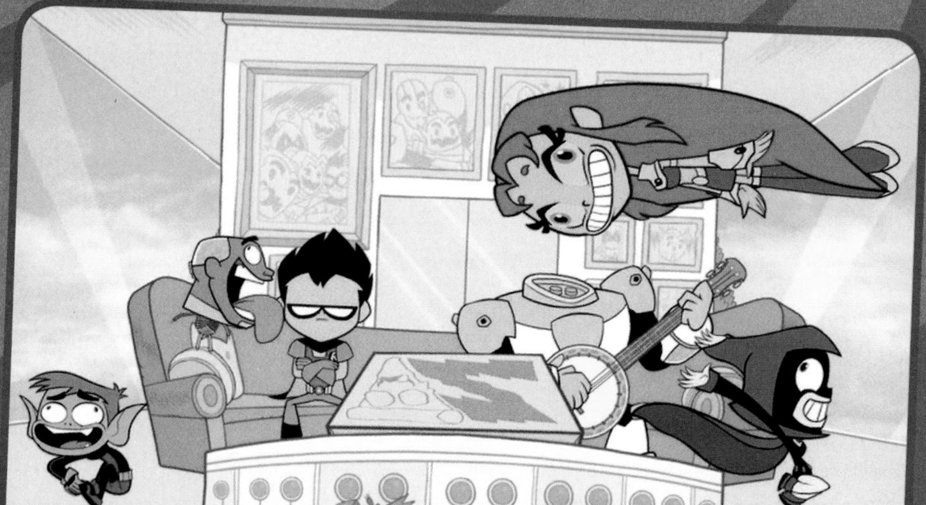

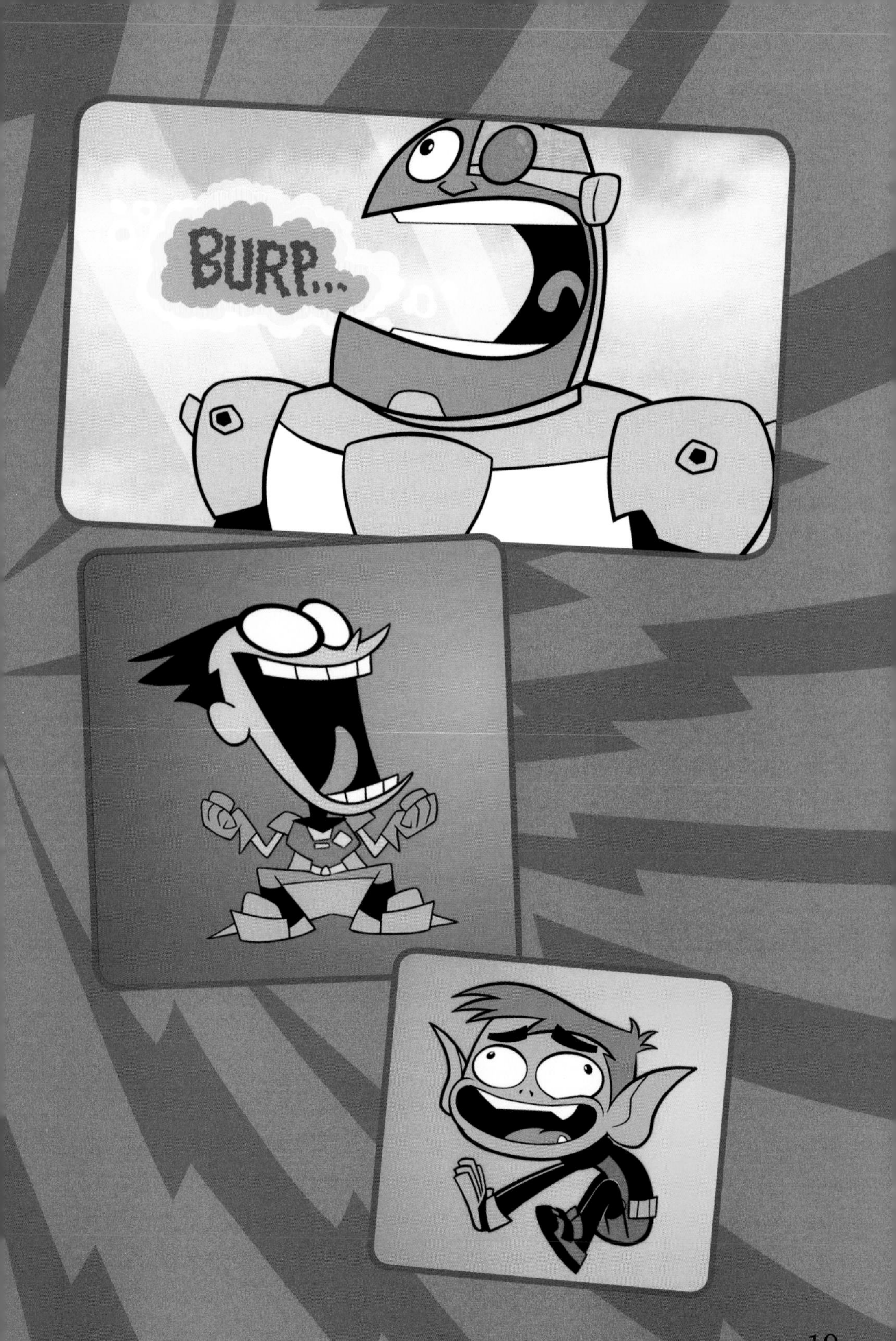
BURP...

Even Silkie
is crazy for pizza.

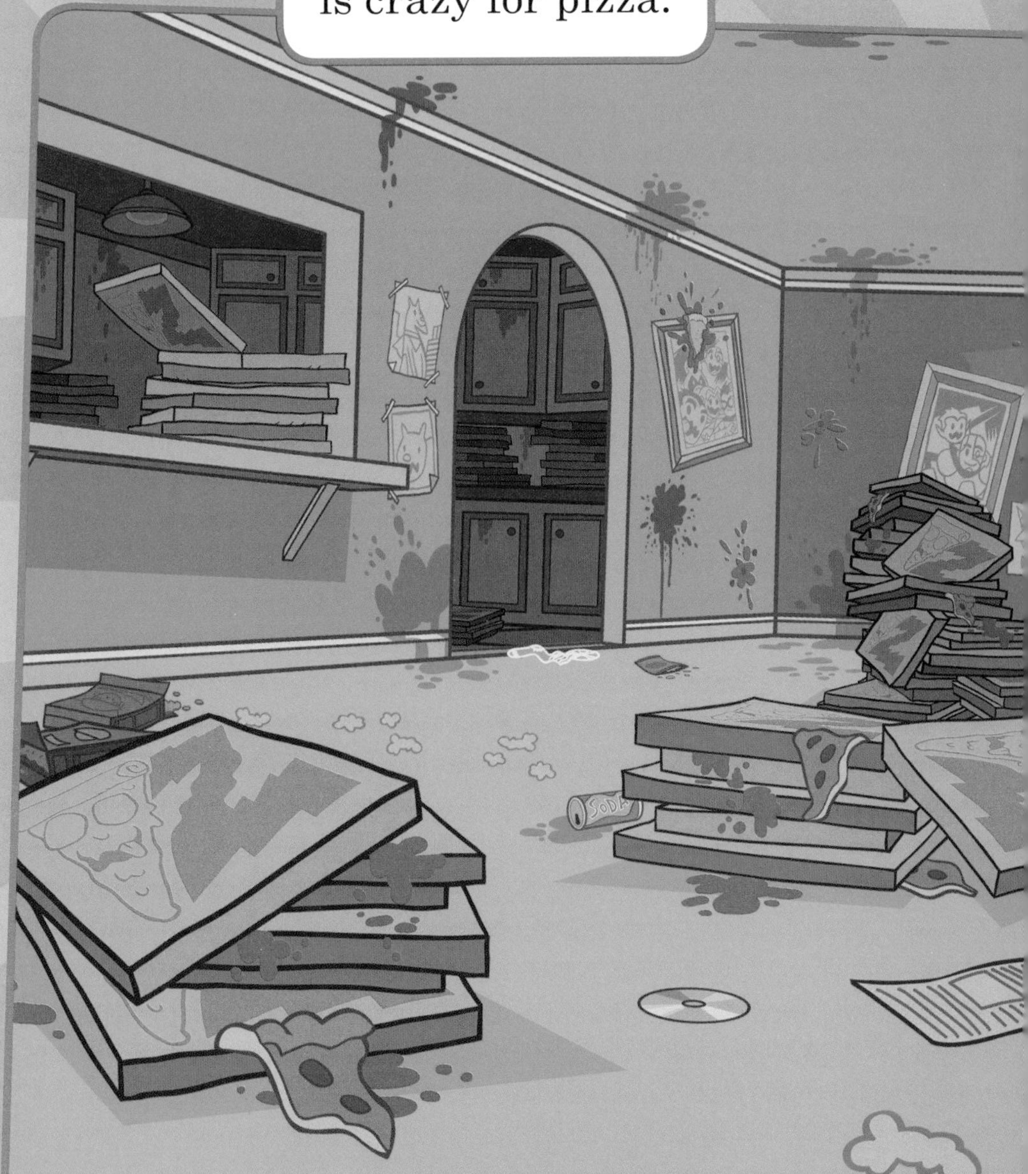
SODA

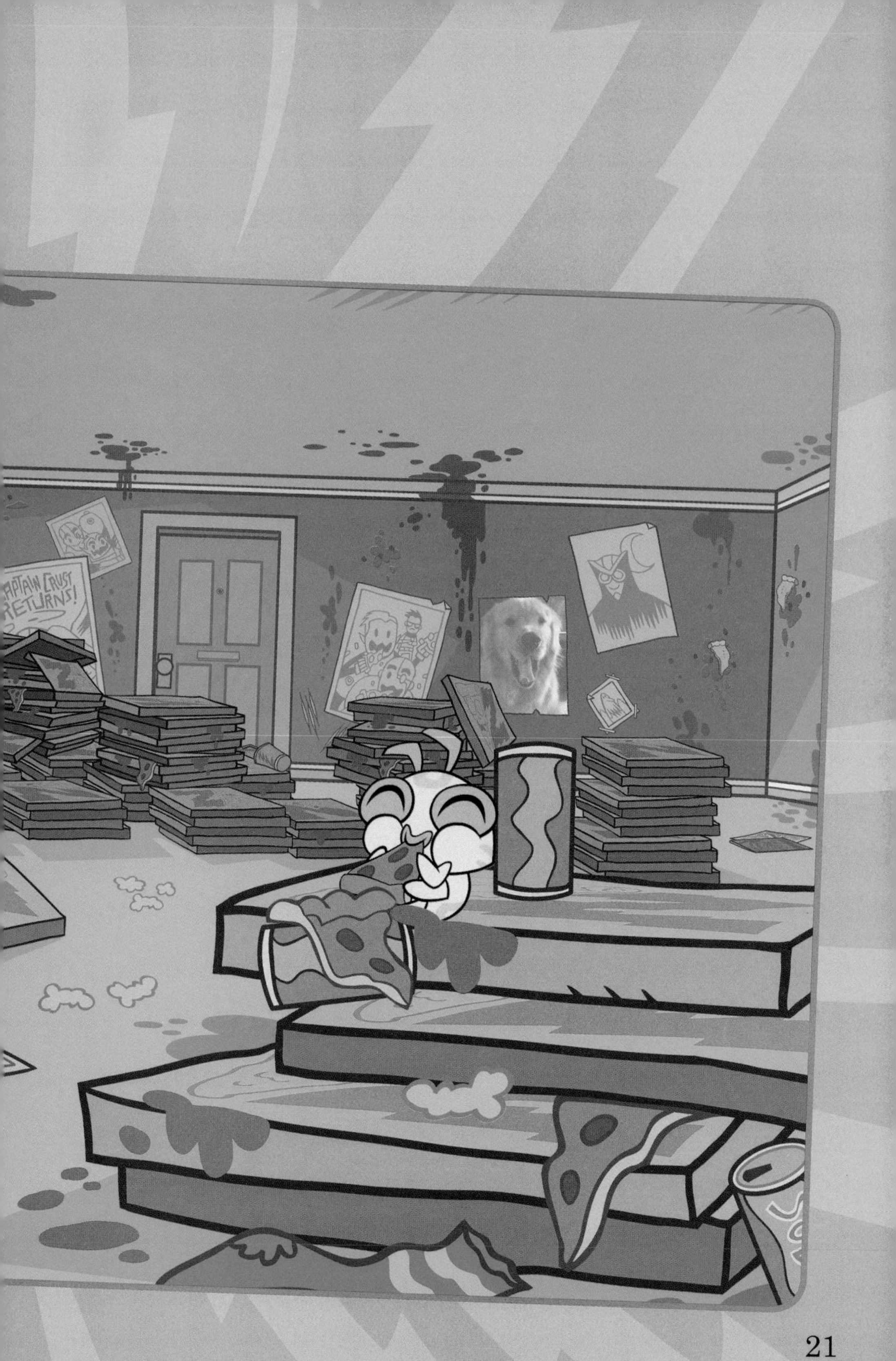
APTAIN CRUST
RETURNS!

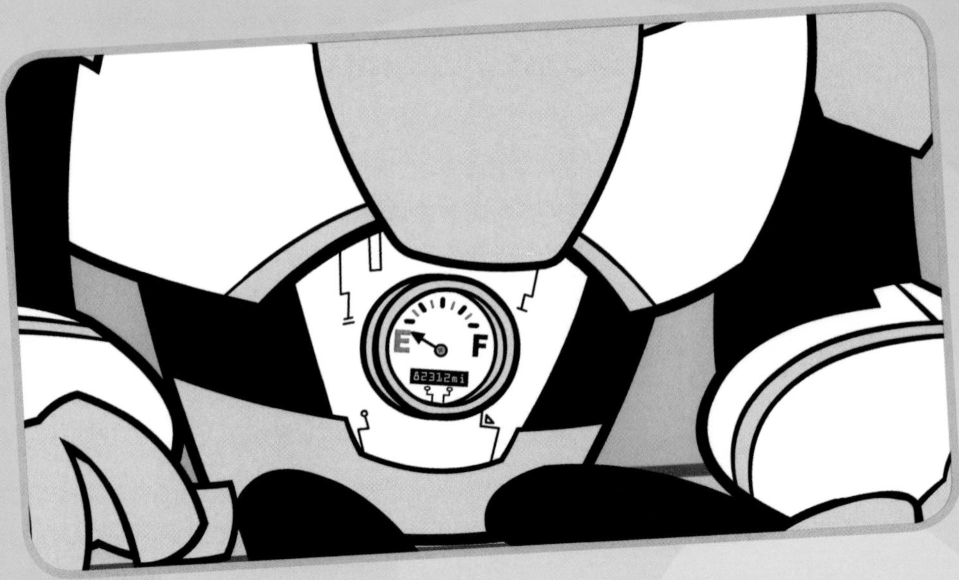
E
F

Cyborg's tank is empty.
"Let us get a pizza,"
says Beast Boy.

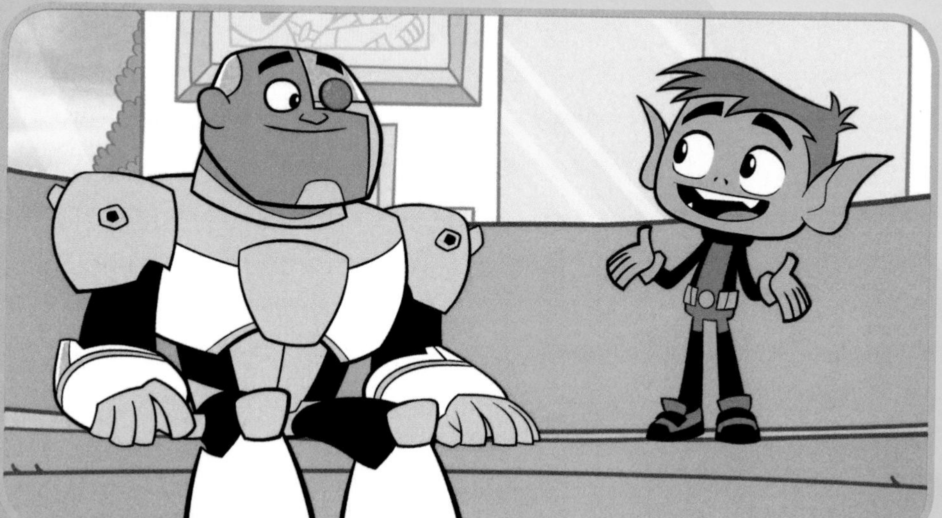

"If it is late,
the pizza is free."

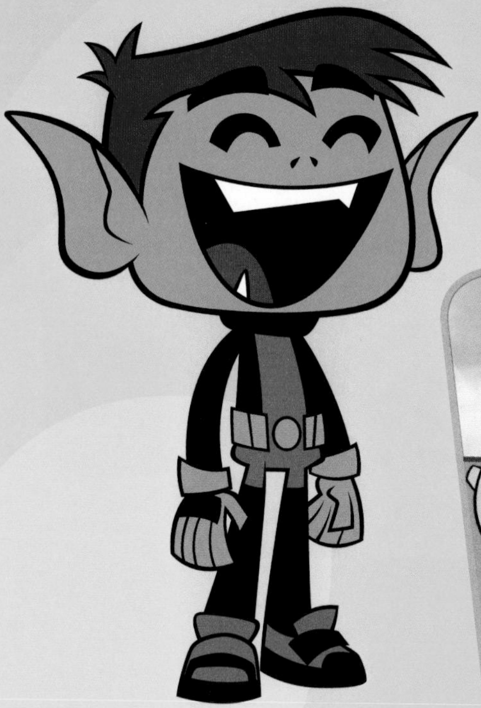

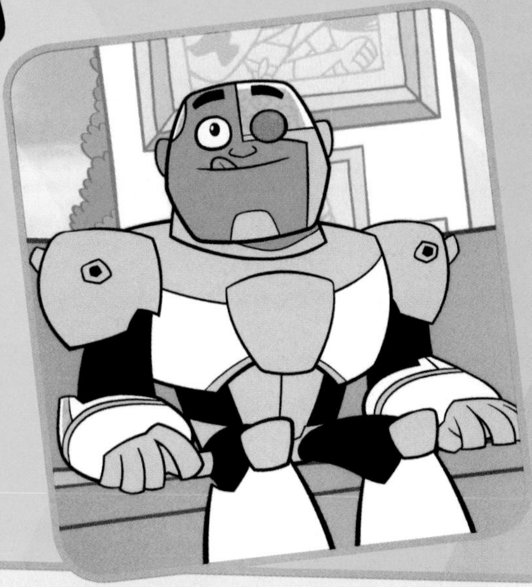

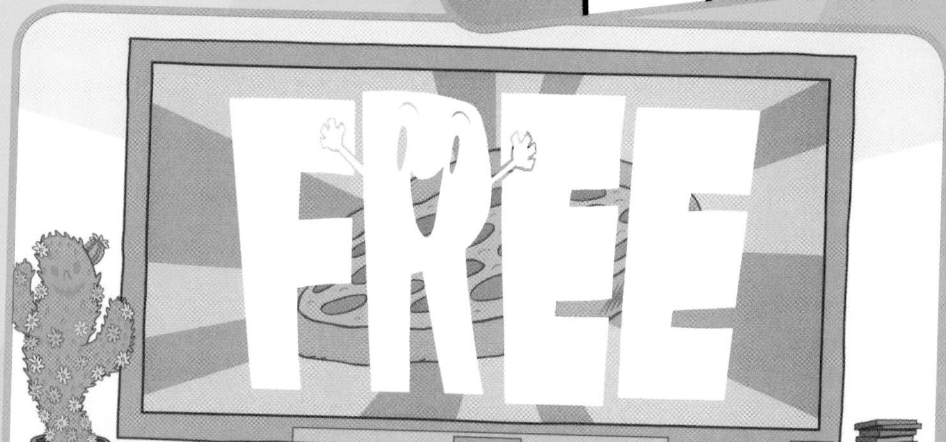
FREE

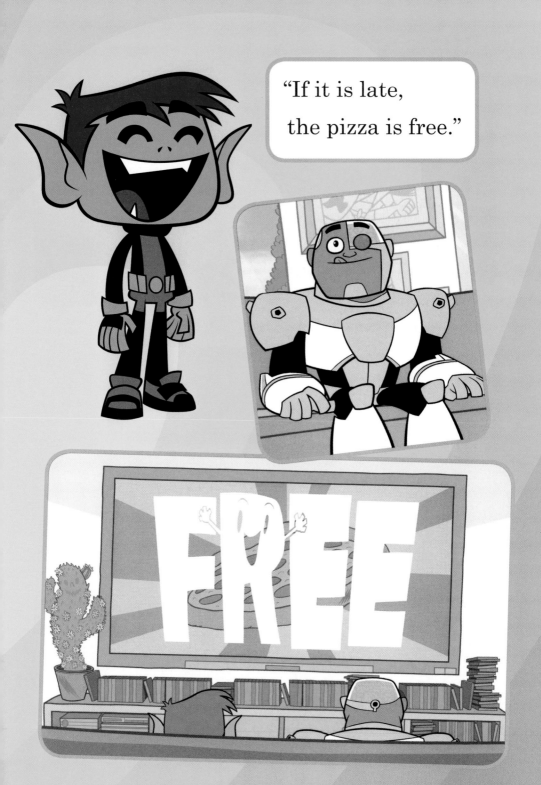

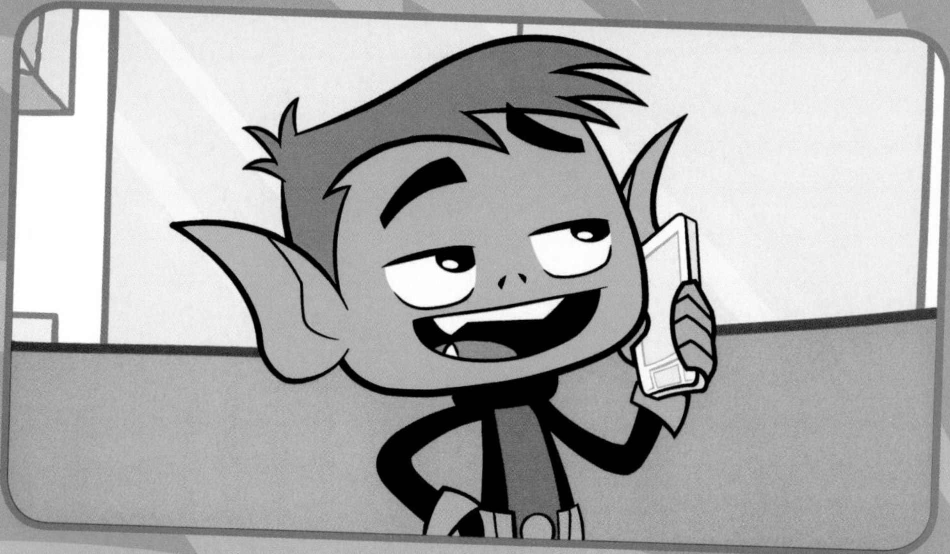

Too bad the pizza guy
is always on time.

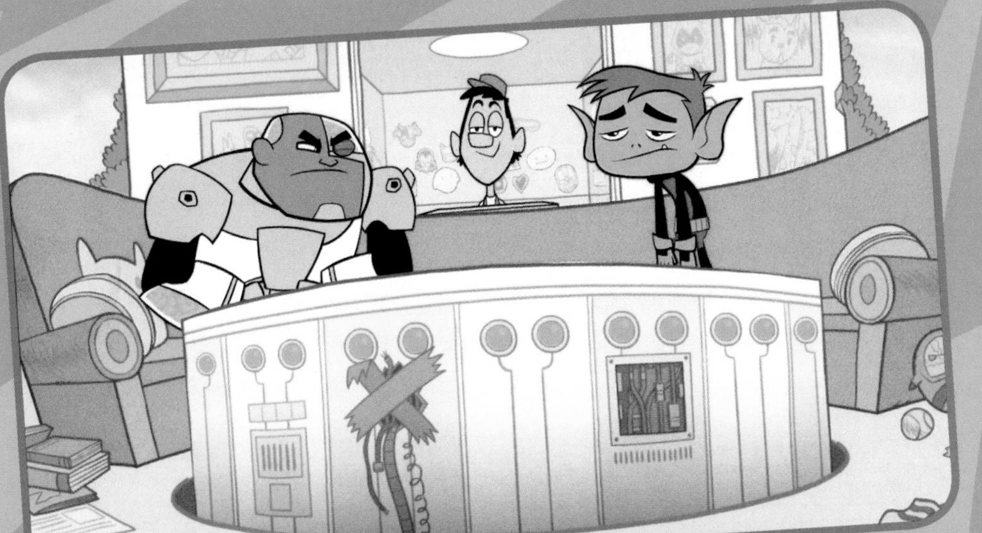

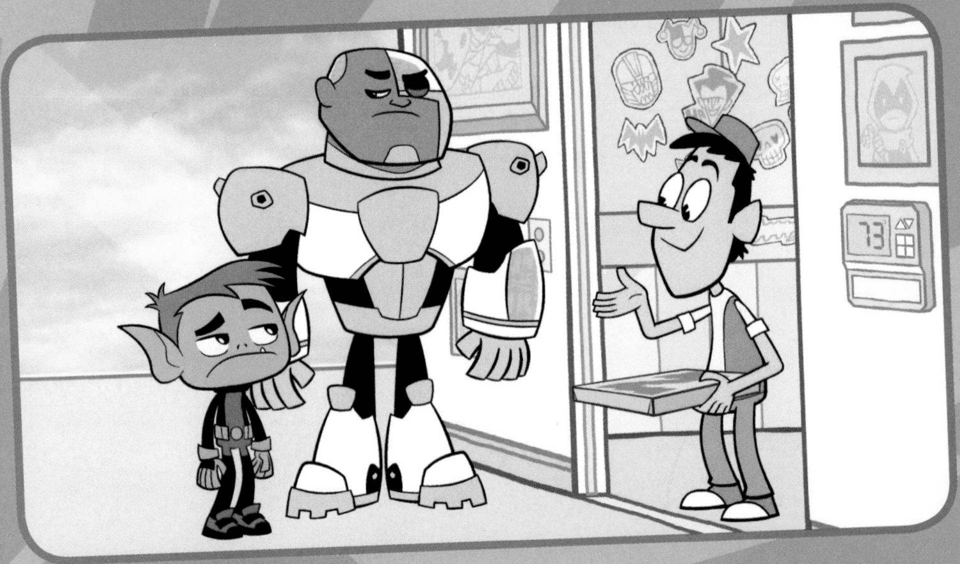

“Hey, pizza!” says the pizza guy.

“Can I pay with a pony ride?” asks Beast Boy.

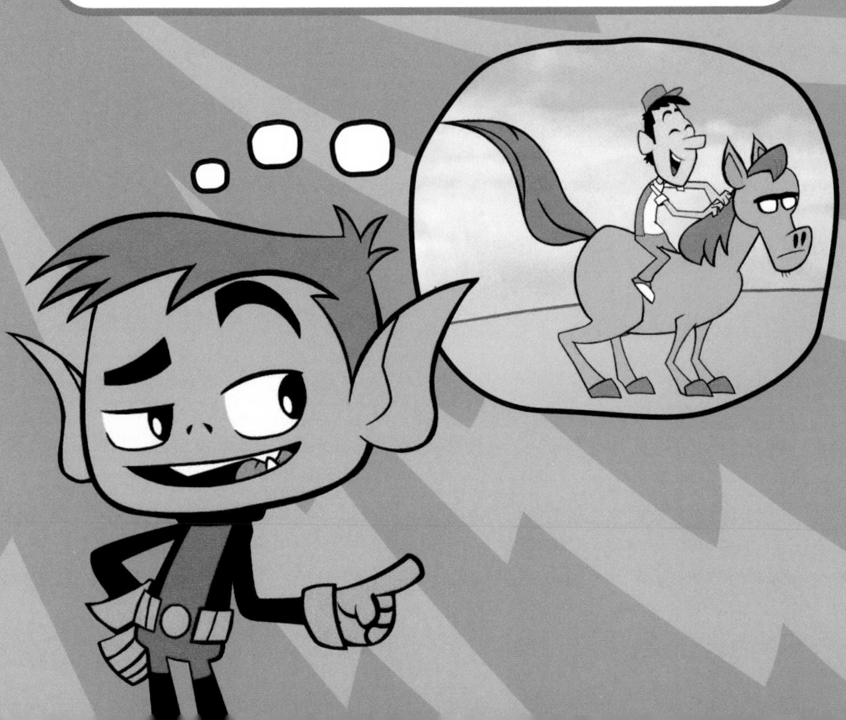

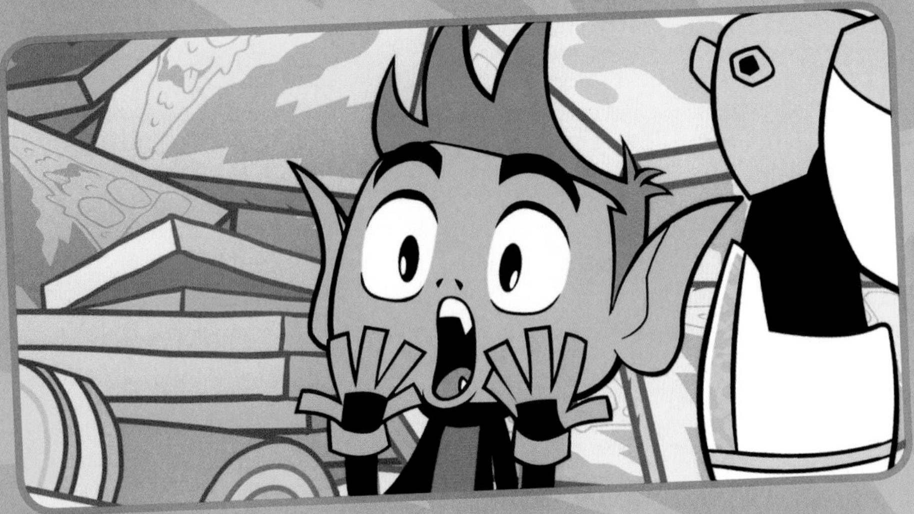

However, there is one
kind of pizza that
scares the Teen Titans.

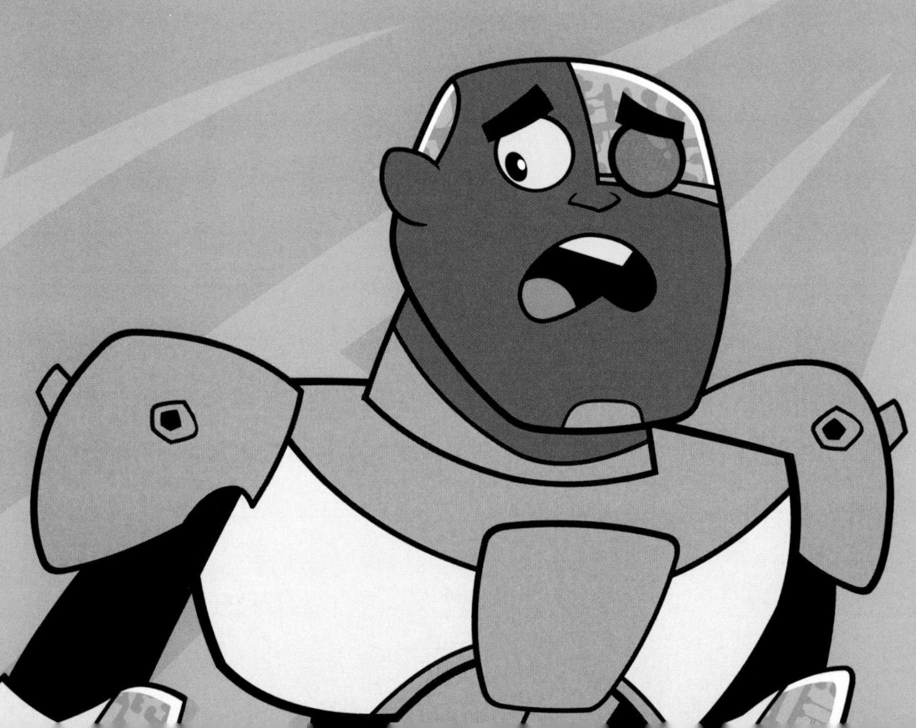

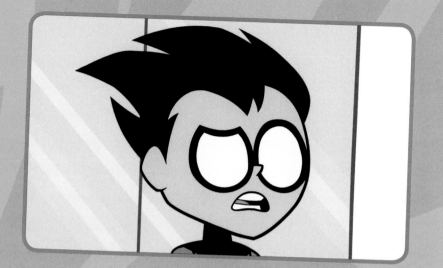

Is it the kind with the weird little fish? No...

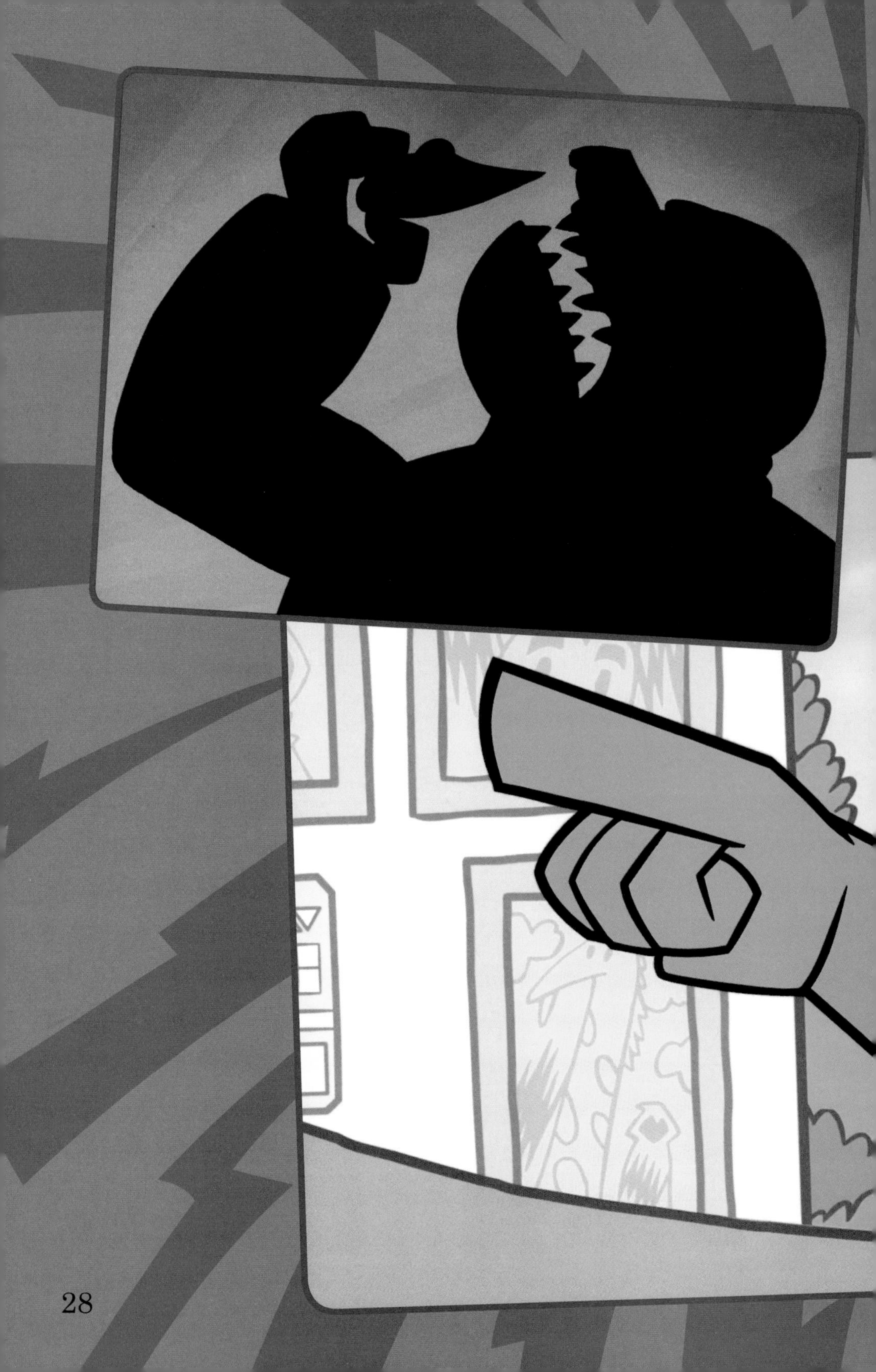

PIZZA MONSTER!!!!

Quick!

Close that box.

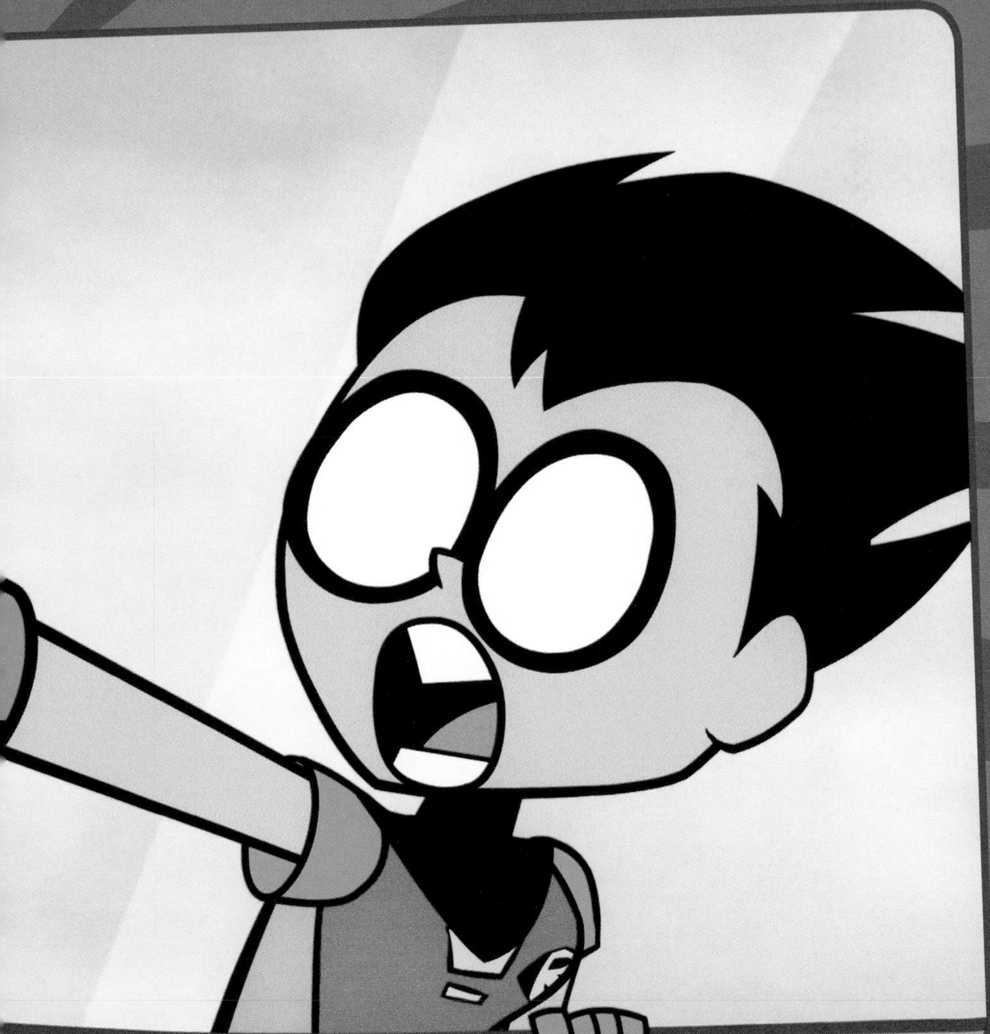

Phew.
That was close.

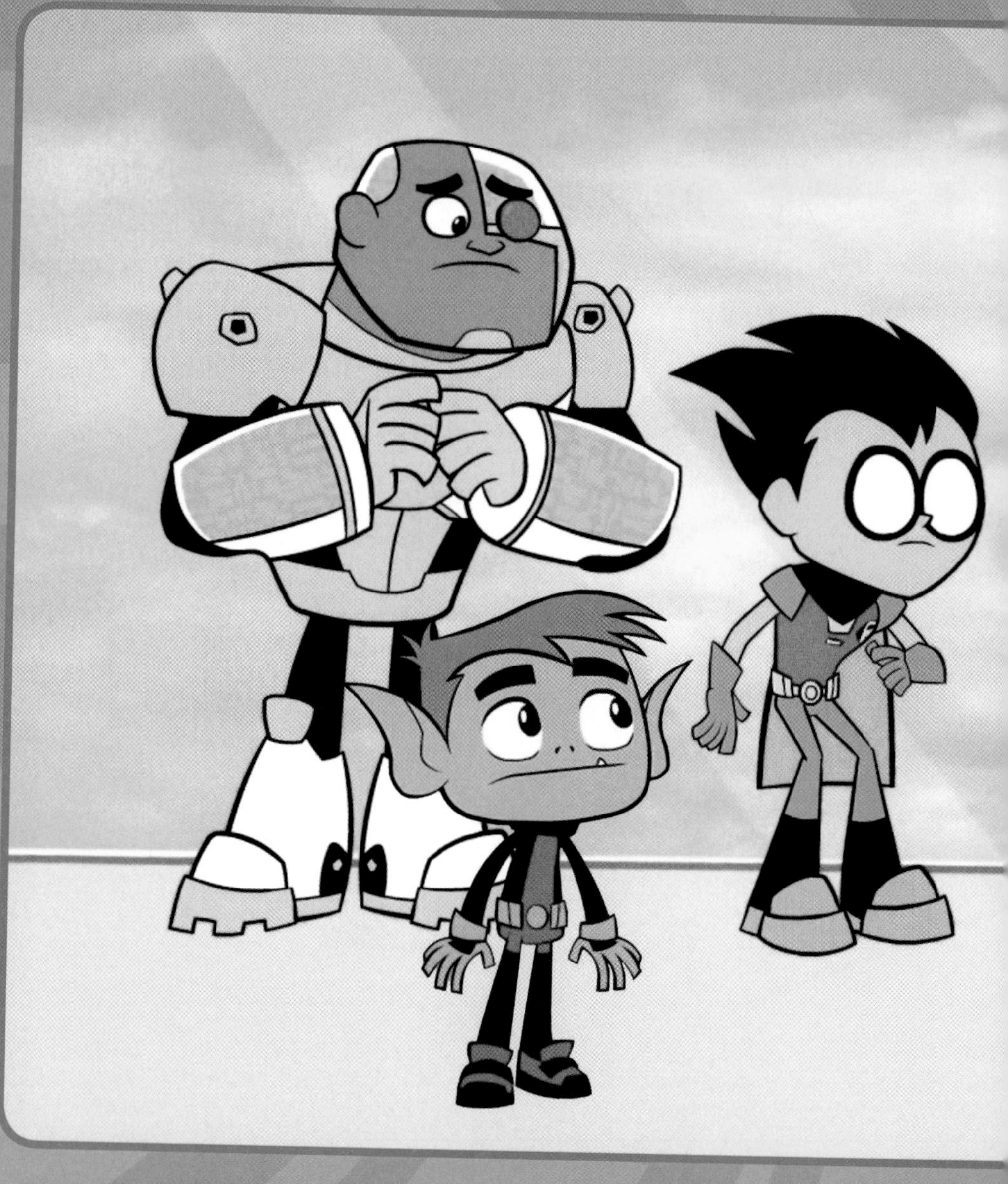

What will the Titans do now?

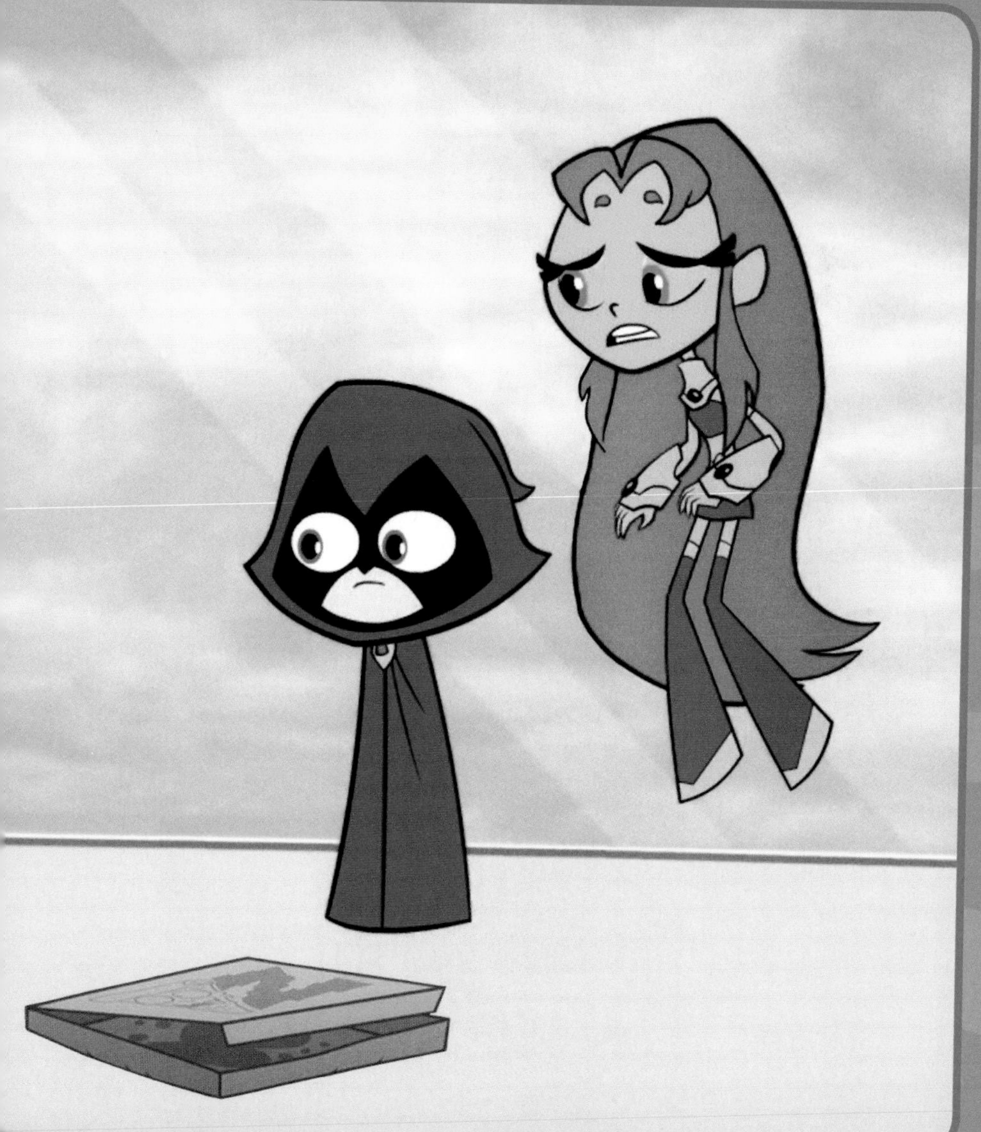

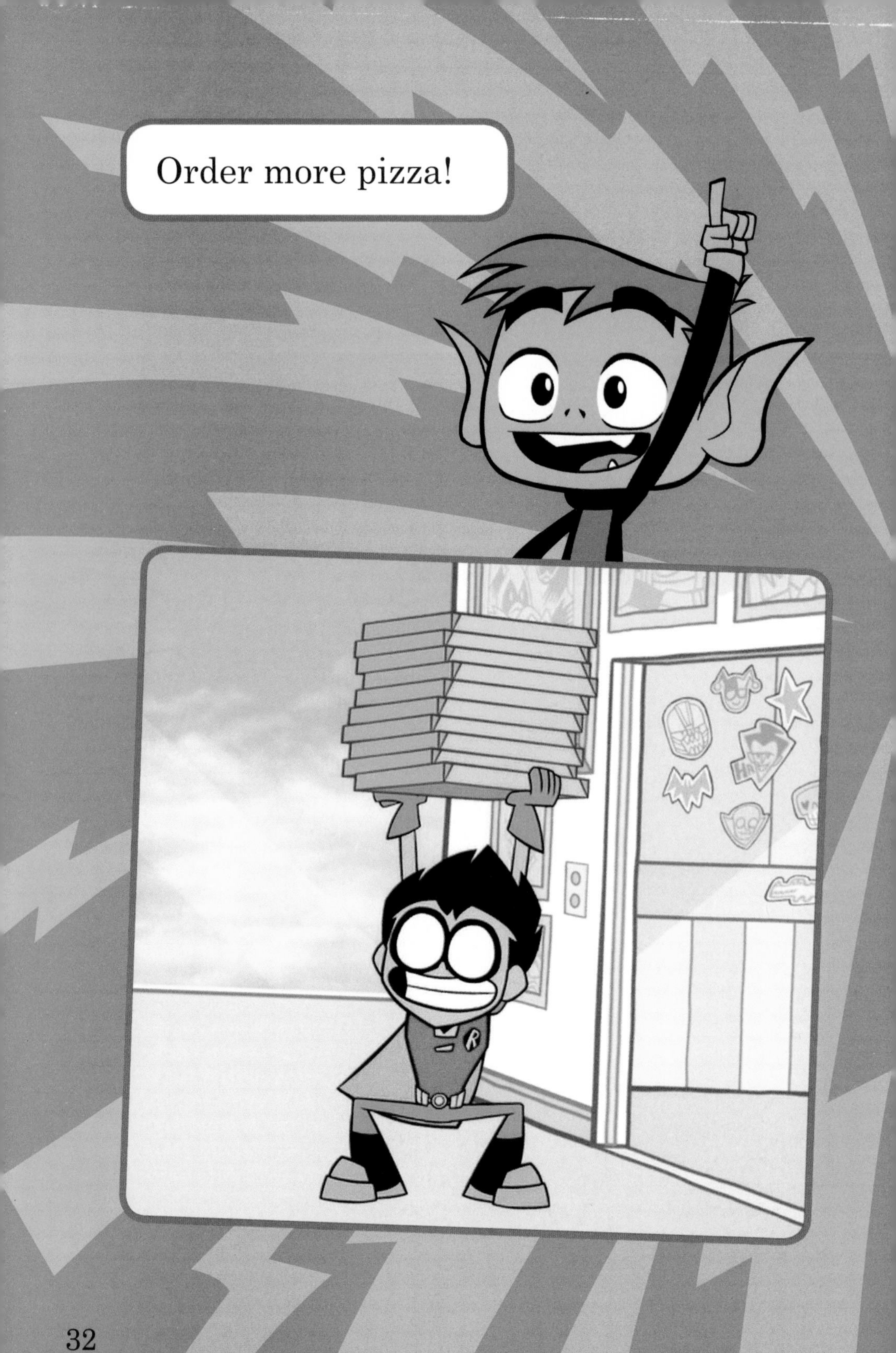
Order more pizza!